NOSTALGIA HAS RUINED MY LIFE

ZARAH BUTCHER-McGUNNIGLE

NOSTALGIA HAS RUINED MY LIFE

FICTION

Published 2021
from the Writing and Society Research Centre
at Western Sydney University
by the Giramondo Publishing Company
PO Box 752
Artarmon NSW 1570 Australia
www.giramondopublishing.com

Designed by Jenny Grigg
Typeset by Andrew Davies
in Tiempos Regular 9/15pt

Cover photograph © Zarah Butcher-McGunnigle

Printed and bound by SOS Print + Media
Distributed in Australia by NewSouth Books

A catalogue record for this book is available from the National Library of Australia.

ISBN 978-1-925818-77-2

9 8 7 6 5 4 3 2

The Giramondo Publishing Company acknowledges the support of Western Sydney University in the implementation of its book publishing program.

This project has been assisted by the Commonwealth Government through the Australia Council, its arts funding and advisory body.

Dedicated to the memory of Patricia Nicolas

Everyone is getting married. I'm eating these disgusting chocolates that have melted and re-formed five times while sitting in my friend's hot car. My sister has fallen in love with a $64 fish. I'm really depressed, maybe I should have a baby. I already feel like a mother though because I've dated a lot of immature people. I think I need to have an emotional experience with a dolphin. I think that would help me, if not a baby. Dolphins always seem happy and like they are smiling. However, the blubber under their skin disconnects facial muscles from skin, so they are actually incapable of facial expressions.

A lot of people have advised me not to focus on romantic relationships and focus on friendships instead but I don't have any close friends. The last time I had a close friend I enjoyed spending time with was when I was eight.

The last guy I dated was still officially married to his ex-girlfriend. He said that he hadn't wanted to get married and he'd told her that he didn't want to get married. But then she proposed and he didn't know how to say no. 'I don't understand,' I said. 'If you didn't want to get married why did you get married.' 'It's not that easy,' he said. 'Have you ever been proposed to?'

From the discomfort of my own home I buy dresses, look up recipes, do online surveys. I woke up to complete a survey to get free food but I didn't qualify. I don't qualify for any of these surveys. I think I should have fallen in love again by now. I put on a choker before eating dinner alone in my room. My mother always asks me if the person I'm dating is 'the love of my life'. Then yesterday she sent me a message that said 'hi I just sent u and your sister an article about the odds of finding love. apparently, it's just a numbers game. if u do nothing it's 1 in 536 on any given day.' I woke up to make a big batch of ice cubes. I want to walk down a very long driveway. I have met someone new but it's too early for them to find out I'm a judgemental petty bitch. I need them to form an emotional attachment to me first.

Unfortunately to get more friends you tend to have to have friends in the first place. To get a job it's easier if you have a job in the first place. The fear of money is affecting my endocrine system. Continental breakfast and bobby pins falling out. I was about to enjoy this cereal but then I remembered I'm not allowed to enjoy anything because I don't have a job.

I go to a group interview and we have to stand in a circle the whole time while the interviewer says things like, 'What kind of fruit would you be and why.' I can't think of a reply but I'm not allowed to leave until I do. I've been seeing a lot of moon boots around lately. I can't remember if I took my medicine. I keep thinking 'why am I doing this' about nothing in particular. Everyone I've dated or had sex with has been a 'dog person' and I hate dogs. Every time I mention to my mother that I'm finding it hard being unemployed she says, 'Why don't you start your own business? I really don't know why you haven't tried to do that.'

My father is getting remarried. The wedding is at 7 a.m. He keeps asking me which brunch option he can put me down for at the restaurant. I say fried eggs on toast. He says, 'Ok I've put you down for eggs benedict.' He asks me what I have been up to recently and I say nothing because I am very depressed and anxious. He says, 'Oh right, well, I am thinking about getting the house renovated because there's no indoor/outdoor flow.'

At the wedding I hug the bride and snag her dress with my fingernail. I bring a rubber plant as a gift. I keep blowing my nose every time someone looks at me so they won't talk to me. But in the middle of brunch my aunt turns to me to say, 'So, do you have any hobbies?' Well, I don't make art anymore, I just have disappointing relationships. All of my emails sound like I wrote them with a knife held at my throat.

The dress I'm wearing smells like mould but it's somewhat comforting. I have five different online dating profiles. I'm not smiling in any of the photos. Someone said they were surprised when they met me because I actually smiled a lot in person. I don't think I'd have the same personality if I didn't have my big eyebrows. I keep taking photos and changing the photos on my profiles. Each week I change half of the photos like how one changes half the water when cleaning a fish tank. Low bone density and big eyebrows are on trend right now, fortunately.

My mother already owned a house by the time she was my age. My father had three degrees and had been married twice. I feel productive changing a photo on my dating profile. I'm using problem-solving skills. I want kids. I'm too bloated to have sex though. I bought an enema kit and bone broth powder. I want my life to begin. I hope no one can tell this is fake leather. I dreamt my depression clothes clogged the washing machine. Water leaked out all over photo albums and game consoles.

I'm angry because I'm so cold and so ugly. I'm bored as soon as I wake up. It was good when I was pregnant because I had a goal and a structure to my life. The end goal was killing the baby but at least I had something tangible to focus on. There's no point having crushes on people though because people aren't that great. My date asked me what I was doing this weekend and I said, 'Wait, what day is it today,' and my date said, 'Yeh I guess all the days blur together when you don't have much going on.'

'Do you want to see the worst photo of me I just took,' I say to my sister. I feel I start conversations with that maybe too often. My friend suggested that M. and I go on a double date with her and Y. She said we should go bowling. I said I couldn't go bowling with my disability. She said, 'Oh.' She said, 'Oh, I don't know what we could really do then, as a double date, if we can't go bowling.'

Woke up to a message from someone I haven't spoken to in a while that said, 'hey so if u could send me nudes that would be appreciated, I'm going to jail soon for 2–3 years.' The only thing I have going for me right now is that I have good nipples and good eyelashes. On the train on the way to a job interview I'm looking at my own nudes to build my confidence. The interviewer asked me what I was doing between 2013 and 2015 and I didn't feel like I could say debilitating depression and poor physical health so I said I worked as an English tutor for an educational company, but then she asked for a reference from them.

I'm very cold and I can't concentrate on anything but also I feel existentially embarrassed about wanting to be warm. The only thing keeping me warm this winter is period blood soaking into my underwear. I finally bought a heater but it is small and doesn't warm up my room properly. Three days later I'm still experiencing cognitive dissonance regarding the heater I bought and the heater that the people at the shop tried to sell me. The heater that would have warmed up my room properly was too expensive because I don't have a job. I want to tell someone I love them but there is no one to tell. Except my sister maybe. I want to pick blackberries on a farm and then die.

My ex-boyfriend messaged me out of the blue to say he got accepted for a drug trial, testing drugs for a disease I have. I don't leave the house all day then I put on a formal/evening wear dress to go to the supermarket. I'm shopping local this year and I'm single. I keep thinking 'please kill me' and 'back to basics'. I buy apples and apple-scented candles. The pain in my jaw makes it difficult for me to bite into apples and to give blowjobs for too long. I have to cut an apple into very small pieces. I thanked my ex-boyfriend in the acknowledgments section of my book but he didn't actually do anything. I talked too much about my ex-boyfriend and my skin condition on my date with the IT guy. When I took off my dress I still said, 'Remember, the rash on my back...it's not contagious, it's just another autoimmune disease.'

I had a brief period last week where I didn't hate everyone. But now I'm back to hating everyone. Someone from an online dating website asks me if I am going to this music festival because everyone he knows is going and he feels left out. 'I've never heard of it,' I say, 'I don't even know what that is.' I say, 'I don't have any friends though so maybe that's why I don't hear about these things.' He says, 'Everyone loves to say they don't have friends when they actually do.' I say, 'Yeh, and everyone loves to say to people who say they don't have any friends, that they actually do have friends because they've never been in a position where they haven't had friends so they can't actually imagine it.' 'Well, your negative energy is probably putting off potential friends right now,' he says.

Eating organic beef sausages with stevia-sweetened tomato sauce while reading my horoscope on astrologyzone.com. Am I the only person I know who doesn't do drugs…? I wish I could sew. I feel like my life would be better if I could sew. But once I did a four-day bookbinding course which involved a lot of sewing and I had a breakdown during the lunchbreak on the second day and had to go home. I can barely afford to pay my rent but I bought a $60 hat which I've been wearing inside for the last three hours. I look the most attractive around 3 a.m. I think. I want people to see me at this hour but also I don't like people staying in my bed. I don't like being touched while I'm sleeping and I don't like anyone facing me while they sleep. I don't care if they are unconscious and their eyes are closed, if they are facing me then I can't relax.

I hated going to my doctor's appointment but at least it got me out of the house. My sister said I should write a list of things I need to do each day and then I should just do them. 'I can't believe I didn't win the contest I didn't enter,' I say, holding a tissue full of chewed-up meat. I tried to reply to an email. I wrote 'hi thanks for your email,' then I had to lie down for two hours. I guess I'll have to slap my own face and my own ass. I stayed up until 4 a.m. trying to write the sixty-word, unimportant email. I feel stressed because 'hi' sounds so passive aggressive but 'hello' seems so formal.

My legs hurt but this is nothing new. I am on medication to help them stop hurting but they still hurt sometimes. My ex-boyfriend said he liked how thin I was because I looked weak. Like he could pin me down easily. I needed pills for the pain in my body, but I worried they'd make me gain weight so I waited a long time before I took them.

Before I went to sleep I changed my Tinder bio to read, 'Don't call looking for casual sex looking for fun, sex isn't fun,' and someone immediately messaged, 'What do you mean sex isn't fun, what is it then? I really feel sorry for you.'

I can't be reheated anymore. I'm wearing my fur coat and animal slippers I stole from a front yard in a small town. Every second person I talk to seems to be a chef. I don't have any plans but I have to pretend I have some. Someone at the art show asked me if I was having fun. I said I'd never had fun in my life. Feeling alienated is only cute if you're pretty. In the abortion operating theatre they were playing that song that goes, 'I believe in miracles...where you from...you sexy thing.'

Everyone's having a closing down sale. The employees aren't bothering to adjust their personality to the customers anymore. Maybe they never did in the first place. I buy a discounted gift for my date. I accidentally litter on the way to his house. 'I like your skirt,' he says. 'It's actually a dress,' I say. He picks at his toenails before touching my clit. He won't open my gift. He says he'll open it later. All the lights on in the middle of the day. He wanted to date me because he felt comfortable with me. He felt comfortable with me because he felt better than me. I feel sorry for him because I know he hates my pity.

When he's fucking me I am thinking about what would be an easy but nutritious lunch option for him. I notice I have four cans of chickpeas next to the bed. He asks me if I have a job yet. When he's going down on me, psoriasis flakes from my thigh fall into his mouth, accidentally. He tells me I can't be picky about work and that I should get a job at the supermarket. 'Or a bookstore, you like books don't you. Or why don't you do a PhD?' He drinks from my breasts. I can see his sacral chakra is weak. But mine is even worse. 'What did you do today?' he asks. I tell him I made a dreamcatcher. He says he's only had two bad dreams in his life.

I named my foetus after a vegetable. So I would feel healthy. Everyone thinks I'm a vegetarian even when they have seen me eating meat at their house. I give off a vegetarian aura. I don't need to buy food but I go to the supermarket for something to do. I only have two friends and I just fell out with one of them. I see the ex-friend at the supermarket. She tells me she is starting a gourmet pretzel company with her daughter. I say, 'That's nice, yesterday I parked illegally to go to a Mongolian BBQ buffet.'

I pour collagen powder into my pumpkin soup. My grey hair makes me look old but my mild acne and small breasts make me look young. I don't care about pleasure. My inflammatory illness makes me look old, but my Furby backpack makes me look young.

'Excuse me, do you realise your skin looks bad?' a supermarket cashier says to me. 'Your skin is discoloured, you look sick,' she says. 'I just thought you should know in case you weren't aware.' I stare at the turkey breast I wanted to buy. 'Thanks, yes, I'm aware,' I say, and walk away without getting my change.

I can see my ex-boyfriend is listening to jazz fusion right now, according to his online music profile. I feel nostalgic for the time he came with me to the emergency department when I couldn't walk. We weren't dating then but when I was coming out of anaesthetic, I told the nurse that despite our difficulties, I was so glad he was there with me right now.

Is the noise I can hear coming from the inside of the building or the outside, I can't tell. No one is replying to any of my messages. Last week I was supposed to go on a date with someone who already cancelled on me twice. The first time he said he was too tired, the second time he said the weather was too warm. I said to him, 'Look, if you have changed your mind about meeting, that's ok, let me know, otherwise we could do Thursday.' He didn't acknowledge the part of the message about changing his mind or not, he just went ahead and made a third plan for Thursday. But when I woke up on Thursday, there was a message from him at 7.50 a.m. that said he couldn't meet up. He said he'd gone to his therapist and realised he wasn't in the right state to meet people at the moment. Well, I could have told you that for free, I wanted to say, but I didn't reply.

What's my goal supposed to be. Someone has buck teeth but it's ok for them because they have an art school fringe and they're a DJ and everyone loves that combination. I'm starved for validation so I'm still focusing on the dopamine boost I got from someone complimenting my pubic hair three days ago. 'Excessively silky' was the descriptor.

I check my horoscope and it says I'm going to have a month of ups and downs. I will go very high up and then very far down. I check the horoscope of someone I no longer speak to. They're having a productive month. 'You can't sit around and do nothing all day,' my mother says. 'You should do an online course.' 'On what?' 'I don't know, something you're interested in.'

I'm in the mood to get a hickey right now. I'm worried my shoes are ugly. 'I was reading an article today,' my mother says, 'about a woman who has no arms and legs and she draws amazing pictures using her mouth. She sold the pictures to raise money for charity. Maybe you could organise something like that, maybe you could do a fundraiser.' 'Yeh maybe,' I say. I think about how I managed to avoid eye contact with everyone for the three years of undergrad. Maybe if I hadn't managed that, my life would be different and better right now. I send my sister a picture of my shoes. 'Yeh, you're right,' she says, 'they do make you look like you have something wrong with you.'

The mystery shopper is ambitious, athletic, with a big dick. I ask him what his Myers-Briggs type is and he says he is an INFP. 'What, INFP, but I'm an INFP. You don't seem like an INFP, I don't know if you actually are one.' 'I am,' he says. 'That's what I got when I did the test.' 'Ok,' I say, 'I'm going to do the test right now and pretend I'm you while I'm doing it.'

I walk the perimeter of the mall. I really want to buy something but I can't find anything to buy. Then I can't find my way out of the mall. I get lost three times. As I am getting lost, someone I know messages me to say they just matched with my ex-boyfriend on an online dating site.

I am late to my job trial. The job trial is in a suburban but industrial part of town. I have to put pasta sauce into fifty plastic bags with a very large ladle and I'm not supposed to get any sauce on the sides of the bags. I am very slow and I keep checking the weight of the bag and trying to scoop up excess sauce back out of the bag with the large ladle which keeps touching the sides of the bag. I'm not a practical person. Two people are watching me and the warehouse we are in has high ceilings and no windows. One of the women watching me says, 'Are you just out of school?' I say, 'No, I'm twenty-eight.' She asks me what I studied at university and I say creative writing and she says, 'Oh, well, that's not going to lead to a job is it.' She criticises the way I am placing spinach on rice. She pulls me aside. 'We're not really sure what you're looking for,' she says.

I take a taxi to the mystery shopper's house. 'Did you get paid for the trial,' he says, and I say no. We lie on the bed. I say my hand is too sore to give him a handjob right now because of the arthritis in my hand. He says, 'You don't look sick, you seem too young to be sick.' I want him to be my boyfriend but he doesn't want to commit. The mystery shopper says, 'Maybe you should be a teacher, I think you'd be good as a teacher and additionally, you already dress like a teacher.' I say I already thought about that. I applied for teacher college and a few weeks after my interview, the interviewer called me to her office and asked me what my plans were for the upcoming year. I said, 'Well, the teaching course? I hope?' She told me I was academically strong, but that I seemed too fragile and submissive to be a teacher. 'Are you sure you want to be a teacher,' she said. 'Why don't we brainstorm some other possible options for you for this year?'

Woke up from a dream about the cupboard my housemate is trying to force upon me. Recently she found this cupboard on the side of the road. 'It would be perfect for you,' she keeps saying, 'You need storage so you can finally clean your room.' But I don't want the cupboard. I don't want another large thing in my room. And it's not the right colour. 'Why can't you just be excited about the cupboard I got you,' she said. 'I'm just trying to help you, if you don't accept the cupboard then I'm never going to try and help you ever again.'

'We can go get dinner. Or we could throw ourselves into the harbour, what do you want to do.' I had bought a cabbage from the grocery store earlier and I still had the cabbage with me. I placed it in the third chair at the table at the restaurant. I don't know what to choose from the menu because everything is dangerous. Everything is mucus-forming. Grains and nuts contain phytic acid which interferes with mineral absorption and meat is high in fat which is bad for the liver and legumes contain lectins which impair digestion.

'You have pretty eyes,' my date says. 'I think you'd feel less depressed if you had a full-time job and didn't have so much time on your hands.' But he's wrong. Every time I've had a job, I've felt more depressed. And I don't feel encouraged when someone says to me, 'You can do it!', I just feel patronised. More than a job I just want someone to love me so much that they write an entire book about me. Or create a whole series of paintings about me.

My date is a good kisser but in the morning when we wake up he just gets out his laptop and sits up in bed replying to emails and booking flights instead of giving me any attention. 'Gotta make money,' he says. His friend also says this to me when I see her in the kitchen. We are at a luxurious apartment in the city where they are dog-sitting an anxious, medicated dog. 'What breed of dog is that,' I ask. 'Why do you want to know, you don't care, you don't even like dogs,' he says.

Watching music videos of this attractive singer who never seems to age. He looks like my ex-boyfriend. Once my ex sent me a picture that he said was him when he was nineteen and I believed him and then he revealed he'd tricked me and it was actually a picture of this singer and I cried. I don't want to watch these videos or read all the comments people have left about how the singer is 'so hot' and they wish they could marry him but I keep watching and reading. I'm scared of my birthday. Two people I have dated told me that women age really badly and that men age really well. Once when I was sitting in bed with someone and we were looking at a fashion magazine from the early nineties, we turned to a spread which showed a crowd of models standing on some stairs. 'Ha, none of those women will be hot now,' he said before he turned the page.

I've been talking to someone from Tinder about hanging out for weeks and then today when I went to confirm the plan he said, 'By the way, I've just fallen madly in love with someone I've been seeing casually for a year, I'm about to ask them to be my girlfriend so I can only see you as a friend, hope that's ok.' I'm looking at a $400 'baked milk lounge dress' on Instagram while on hold to the unemployment office. All my targeted ads are for scientology and not drinking during pregnancy. My mother called me and said, 'Ok I did a depression test pretending to be you and the results said to seek help urgently.' My arms hurt a lot today. It hurts to pick up the phone. I placed a potato next to my pillow. I read that sleeping with a potato can help pain. And potatoes can also absorb negative emotional energy. No one's ever done a post on social media about it being my birthday…I feel like this happens a lot for other people. Someone will be like, 'Hey it's my girl Laura's birthday today! Love her!' with a picture of them from three years ago or something. I only got three hours sleep but I need to apply for a job. Applying for jobs is so hard though because as soon as I read 'attach your cover letter' I think…fuck I can't be bothered, I don't care about this at all…

They were about to alter my skirt to make it smaller but then realised the elastic wouldn't have any elasticity left in it if it was tightened anymore. I had planned to wear the skirt to the dinner with my high school bully. A friend of a friend said she had someone who might have a job opportunity for me. That someone turned out to be the high school bully. While waiting outside the restaurant, I read an article called 'Why I staged my own meltdown on Instagram for art'. She arrives and I see she has the same personality as she did at school, but she doesn't seem to remember me. The bartender somehow squirts lemon juice into my eye while making my drink. In the booth I can't concentrate because my back is facing the door...bad feng shui. My high school bully is confused by the gaps in my CV. She tells me about her makeup and healthcare business, which I quickly realise is a kind of pyramid scheme, though she seems unaware of this. She keeps using the phrase 'at the end of the day'. She talks about how empowered she feels and how much her life has improved and changed. She's spending around $200 a week on skincare products. All of the products have names like 'sunrise joy serum'. I say I'm not sure about joining the business. 'Yeh but how's your plan going?' she says. 'Are you happy with your life?'

I look at wedding dresses online. I don't even want to get married. I think I'm being ignored by someone. I just want to be told I'm being ignored so I know for sure. I can think of treatments that might help my health but to be able to work more to pay for them, I'd have to be healthier. The person who's ignoring me said he thought I'd be a bad driver. His idea of a date was going to the mall so I could help him choose new glasses. I named his cat though, he'll be reminded of me for the next twenty years. On the way to the supermarket I passed a bridal shop and went inside. 'I'm in a wedding shop,' I messaged my ex-boyfriend. 'I want to put bits of salmon under your eyelids on your wedding day,' he replied. 'Can I help you,' the shop assistant said. I said I was getting married in a few months. She asked what venue we had booked. I said my fiancé and I were planning on something low-key in his parent's garden because they had a pond and marquee and everything, but I still wanted a nice dress. She said if I wanted to try on dresses, I'd need to make an appointment. 'Ok sure, when's your next available appointment,' I said.

Couldn't make a decision about a very basic simple thing so eventually did an online tarot reading to help me decide. Now I'm getting fingered surrounded by stuffed animals. I keep seeing his face as a clown's face. Did I see him as a clown somewhere before we met. His dick looks like a slug. He brought me food he found in a bin. He's rich but his household does dumpster diving because it's fashionable. I start to tell him a funny and detailed anecdote about my childhood. He says, 'Sorry I was half asleep, I just missed the last thing you said. Also I'm just not that interested in what you're saying.' 'Ok,' I say. 'Are you upset?' he asks. 'I was just being honest.' Later his head is resting underneath my chin while I hug him. 'I kind of feel like a baby lying like this,' he says. I say, 'My ex used to pretend to be a baby, he would lie with his head in my lap and talk in a baby voice.' 'Oh ok.' 'I'm not saying you have to do that, I'm just saying that's what he used to do.'

On the way home from the hospital he asks me if I've been thinking about our relationship. I'm eating a carrot wrapped in plastic wrap. 'Not really, I've been thinking about the abortion,' I say. When I felt nauseous the nurse asked me if I wanted a biscuit and I said, 'No it's ok, I have a carrot in my bag.' He says his biggest fear is being involved with someone who really likes him and who is in love with him when he doesn't feel the same way. 'I'm just really worried about hurting people,' he says. I throw the carrot nub out of the window. 'Don't worry, I'm not in love with you,' I say. 'I probably have the capacity to love you in the future though, I can see it as a possibility.' 'Ok good,' he says. 'Same, I don't love you either but I can imagine maybe loving you one day.'

I feel productive taking out the empty cracker boxes and some of the dirty dishes in my room. Then I remember this isn't productive because most people don't have ten empty cracker boxes and twenty different mouldy plates in their room. Someone I loved once put their fingers in their ears while I was crying. I'm bored of myself too. I go to an interview for a babysitting job and they start digging a grave for their dying dog while I'm there. 'Did you help dig,' my ex-boyfriend asks. 'I bet you didn't.' 'Haha no, I didn't,' I say. 'But I have a disability, I wouldn't have been able to manage it.' 'I hope one day you're healthy enough to dig a grave,' he says.

Kitten heels in the mud. I wish meditation and prayer were easier. I tried to listen to some relaxing music and started hyperventilating. When I went home with him, I felt like I had to tell him what was wrong with me. 'I have this illness, I have to be careful with my legs,' I said. I thought I heard him say 'So do I,' but he actually said 'Don't worry.' 'Have you ever done one of those online tests to see if you're a psychopath? Sometimes I think I am one. I haven't cried in over seven months.' I said I hadn't done one. He said he didn't know if other people thought in the same way as he did. I said going to a therapist might be a good start if he thought he was a psychopath. 'Oh I have been to therapists,' he said. 'I don't genuinely believe I am one, but I would be interested to find out.'

On a late night ad for a mop, they make a smiley face out of BBQ sauce and eggs and mop it up easily. Everyone keeps asking me if I'm a student and I have to keep saying no and they keep looking disappointed and confused. I wish I had some skills. I want to mop up BBQ sauce and eggs. I want to sweep dust into a pile.

My ex-boyfriend sends me a picture of him wearing an adult diaper. 'I think I'm sending you a video now too,' he says, 'it should be loading.' 'I'm not sure I want to see the video right now,' I say. He says he ate ice cream and is now experiencing a sugar crash from the ice cream. I ask what flavour ice cream and he doesn't answer. I ask again what flavour and he says he's not going to tell me because it isn't important and it wasn't the flavour he would normally choose because the flavour he would have normally chosen wasn't available. I say, 'Well but it is important because I want to know, I like to know details. I'm not going to judge you on the flavour,' I say, 'I just want to know.' Finally he says, 'Ok, it was two scoops, one was almond brittle and the other was strawberry cheesecake.' He says he could only eat half of the ice cream before he threw it away because it was too sweet. 'So what do those flavours say about me then,' he says.

Wake up, eat berries, put lubricating eyedrops into the guinea pig's cloudy eyes which are 'turning to bone' according to the vet. It has become addicted to the strawberry-flavoured tramadol. Last night at a comedy show, one of the comedians asked the audience if anyone knew what faecal transplants were and me and my Tinder date were the only ones who put our hands up. We didn't talk to each other for the rest of the night though. In the foyer I saw someone I knew from university. 'Hey, you're looking well,' she said. 'How are you?' I said I hadn't actually been that well recently, I'd started a new medication. 'Well, you look good anyway, that's the main thing!' she said. In the bathroom the long velvet tie from my dress fell into my ass crack.

He thinks I'm about to give him a blowjob but I'm just bending down to tie my shoe. 'Can we go for a walk in the cemetery?' But he won't go anywhere with me unless I promise we can stop at a bakery or pizza place first. On the internet I read 'when you consume a carbohydrate that has been cooked it has the same effect on your body as white sugar' and my heart rate increases a little and I start sweating. I'm waiting for him to finish a computer game so we can go out. He doesn't need to play the computer game right now. My symptoms of depersonalisation disorder are really strong right now. 'My symptoms of depersonalisation disorder are really strong right now,' I say to him. He says, 'Oh.' I want him to respond more than 'oh' and because he isn't responding anything more than 'oh' my symptoms increase. On a self-help forum I found for depersonalisation disorder, they use the abbreviation 'DP' instead of typing out the name in full. I've started using this abbreviation when I am mentioning it in conversation. 'I feel really anxious because of the DP,' I say. But he says, 'DP? Double penetration? Sorry I can't think of anything else but double penetration when you say DP.' We finally leave the house. I watch him eat a pastry and three quarters of a pizza. We wait so long for the pizza that it's too late to walk in the cemetery.

In my dream I hugged my grandmother and told her, 'You're one of my most favourite people ever.' We were at her old house with the huge balcony. I used to make my ex-boyfriend drive to the old house sometimes and we'd park and stare at it for a while in the dark. It seems like I should live there, that I should find a way of living there one day.

The person I was supposed to meet tonight called me during their lunchbreak to tell me they couldn't meet up now because they needed to do laundry. And they were going on holiday soon, so I couldn't see them until they got back. I said I felt stressed when they took days to reply to my messages. 'Oh I'm flattered I'm making you stressed,' they said. 'You must really like me.'

The therapist has a bandaid on top of his bald head. When I walk in and sit down he says, 'Oh, usually the practitioner sits in the seat closest to the door in case the patient goes crazy and the practitioner has to make a quick getaway, but you don't seem too crazy haha.' He says, 'Tell me about your lifestyle, your work, what you do for fun. What do you do for fun?' 'I don't know,' I say. 'What do you do on a Friday night?' he says. 'I don't do anything,' I say. I say I don't have a job but I can't think of a job I want to do anyway. 'But if you did know, what would you want to do?' He says he is a former comedian, he worked as a clown in an old people's home for years and then decided to become a psychologist. He looks at the notes from my GP. 'Oh that's interesting, I haven't seen that disorder for a while haha,' he says. 'And you do writing. You're an interesting character, I can't quite work you out, it's like trying to fit a square peg into a round hole.' He asks about my writing. I say I haven't been writing, I feel too depressed to write. 'Oh yeh, I get writer's block too,' he says. 'Hang on, I've got the perfect quote about this.' He goes over to his computer and starts clicking on things. 'Sorry, taking a while to find it, but it will be worth it!' He finally finds the inspirational quote and reads it out and it isn't worth it, it's about how you are a vessel for this divine creative gift and it isn't your place to judge the quality of the work that passes through you, it's just your job to keep the channel open and if you can do that then it makes you better than everyone else. 'What do you think about that?' he says. 'I can give you a printed copy if you want, I've got a copy above my desk at home.' He says if I can just channel my pain into art then I'll be ok. 'Pain and suffering are very good for creativity,' he says. 'Look at Kurt Cobain, he wrote all these angsty journal entries when he was a teen and then they became the basis for Nirvana songs which made him millions.'

I'm ovulating. No one's giving me any attention so I make an apple pie at midnight. I spray multi-purpose cleaner on the pie and it shines and then it gets soggy. Last week I had sex with an orphan. But we fell out before I could give him his birthday gift. A candle melted down to make another candle. He was angry I left his house because I felt anxious. 'But I feel pretty terrible too,' he said. 'Can you recommend me some mainstream narrative fiction.' He didn't understand why I was going to the hospital to see my grandmother when I already had plans. He thought it was too much for people to expect you to help them.

I got fired from the nanny job because I fell asleep on their sofa for five minutes. I fell asleep because I was depressed. The girl didn't even notice, she only knew because when I woke up I said, 'Oh I think I might have just fallen asleep.' When I'd offered to buy her a hot chocolate on the way home from school she said, 'Don't waste your money, you can't afford it.' I called my mother to tell her I felt hopeless because I couldn't even keep a nannying job and she started talking about an article she'd read on fire danger, and how it takes forty-five seconds before it's too late to get out once a fire starts. I want skinned knees right now. Now I want scabs on my knees.

Late to my appointment because my ex-boyfriend was like, 'Do you want to scam Airbnb with me, you can make a hundred dollars out of this.' I colour-coordinated my outfit to my medication. I want something to bite me. On the way home my phone falls out of my hand and breaks. I tell my housemate about my broken phone and she says, 'Oh that's difficult when you are poor and you can't afford to replace it.' Last year I went on a date with a 56-year-old man from a sugar daddy website. I got paid a hundred dollars to talk to him while he ate lunch at the botanic gardens café. He asked me if I knew what a 'gif' was. A bird kept jumping on the table trying to get his food and he got really stressed about it. I took photos of the bird.

I tell my friend I'm stressed because I can't afford to buy food for the next few days. He says, 'Yeh me too, same, I only have X amount of money in my account until I get paid tonight.' But he just moved to London and he lives rent-free with his dad and he has a full-time job. I tell him about how my shoe started breaking when I was just sitting down looking at a computer, and then it fully broke, the sole came off completely. I had to travel home for an hour without shoes. He says, 'Oh yeh, me too, my shoe is breaking too, I'm just waiting for it to break fully before I get it repaired.'

I think my ex and I got on because we had both been bullied at high school but not so severely that we couldn't socialise now, but enough to make us humble and to make our self-esteem a bit low. I want to date someone who has been bullied so their self-esteem is a bit low and therefore they won't leave me because they don't think they can do better than me, but not so low that they're self-destructive and self-loathing and unable to accept someone liking or loving them.

I'm trying to have fun but it's very stressful. I'm always running late and because of the pain in my legs I can't run to the station and I miss my train. My housemate says, 'You wouldn't have to run if you just left on time and caught the earlier train.' At the book launch a woman with a pixie cut and expensive brogue shoes tells me I shouldn't apply for jobs that I don't want to do and then I'd never be stuck doing a job I hated. She works at a bookshop and does editing work for a university publishing press. Everyone at the book launch looks like they weren't bullied at high school.

I have a job interview because I went on a date with a guy and his wife a few weeks ago. He invited me back to their place and I said I wasn't sure if I should go. 'I'm pretty tired, I think I left my medication at home too,' I said. He said there was no pressure from them but also that he could get me an interview at his old workplace because he knew I'd been looking for a job for ages. 'The job thing doesn't have any relation to coming to our house though,' he said. I followed them to their train stop.

He smiled and touched my thigh and said, 'You don't have AIDS, do you, tell us now if you do.' I was lying in-between him and his wife. He kept pestering me to tell him what my sexual fetish was. I finally told him because I thought it would create intimacy, but he just made fun of me. He made fun of me also when he asked me to put on music. I put on *Feels* by Animal Collective, and he laughed at the album being called *Feels*. 'You're really cute though, I don't know why you're single. Maybe because you don't have a five-year plan?' I was really hungry and didn't know where to look. I had mentioned being hungry on the train and the wife said she would make me muesli when we got to their house. When she brought out a bowl for me it had the tiniest amount of oats in it but I felt too embarrassed to ask for more.

All of the plants in my room are fake. I have two fake trees in pots (one of them is as tall as me) and a fake potted palm and also a bunch of fake vines. Some people have questioned why I don't just have real plants but the fakeness is beautiful and appealing to me. My dream is to have ten fake trees in my room, around my bed, creating a grove that has this 'otherworldly' feeling. I got the fake palm the first day I moved here and I brought a fake vine with me in my luggage. My ex in my hometown thought the vine was actually real at first. Well, I think he thought it was real for weeks. Once he told me he bought a vine for his room because he was inspired by mine and I said, 'You know it's fake right?' and he hadn't realised.

I got the job. I have a job now. 'Wow you must be so excited,' my mother says. 'I don't know,' I say. 'Come on, please be happy about this,' she says. It's hard to be excited when I don't believe in the future. The interviewer asked me why I wanted an admin job at a bakery when my CV said I studied writing. I tried to pretend I was good at admin, even though I didn't go to the graduation ceremony with the rest of my writing class because I didn't fill out the form and do the admin on time. I can't concentrate on anything because I keep imagining my ankles gnawed open and bleeding, bones exposed. I don't know why I keep imagining this. I feel embarrassed to expect someone to give me money for making phone calls. It's so embarrassing to buy food. It's so embarrassing to hoard money to buy a car, or go on holiday. I eat a bag of chips and feel sick and watch videos of me kissing my ex-boyfriend and videos of us having sex. I don't feel that sexual towards them, it's just documentation. I like to have records of things.

Cum hitting the psoriasis on my elbow made my elbow sting. His ex had psoriasis too, maybe that was his type. I found out she had psoriasis from her blog and I'd scrolled through the entire blog all the way back to the beginning. I asked him to say goodbye to me before he went to work but he didn't, when his alarm went off he left the room quickly and didn't come back in. I had work later in the day at my new job I hated. I've hated every job I've had though. I never managed to find one I didn't hate, I just fantasised about getting into a car accident and being able to sue someone or else starting a petting zoo with my ex-boyfriend as a way to make money instead.

When I got to work there was a message on the answering phone from a customer who said the slices of the multigrain bread they got were too thin and stuck together and difficult to use. Also, the ciabatta rolls were too hard and someone had hurt their gum. I imagined the person hurting their gum and laughed. I printed out my phone list. The sales manager came into the room. He was wearing Crocs and a Hawaiian shirt. 'Do you want to see something special...' he said. 'Ok,' I said. 'Come this way.' He took me downstairs to a small locked room. 'Wait, hang on, let me turn on the light...Ok...Come in.' He proudly revealed a desk set up with eight Christmas gingerbread houses covered in icing and lollies. 'Aren't they beautiful,' he said. 'Pretty good,' I said.

I finally get ringworm. Something new in my life. I arrange to meet someone from an online dating site and we decide to meet in the park. It's night. He messages me to say he's in the field. I ask which field. I say I'm near a field too, the one near the pond. He says he can't see a pond and that he's walking up a hill now. 'I think I see you,' I say. 'I think I just waved at you,' he says. 'I can't see you now though, where did you go?' I reply that I'm not going to wave back just in case it's not him even though I think it is. We meet at the swings. We sit on the swings but there's only one adult swing. He says he'll try and sit on the child's swing. I talk about past relationships even though everyone tells me to avoid talking about past relationships on a first date. He tells me about a horror film he's making about suburbia. 'Do you want half a plum, I have a plum in my car,' he says. I say I have an apple in my bag so he should save the plum for himself. He comes back from the car with a cigarette in his mouth. 'Are you sure you don't want half a plum,' he says, pulling the plum from his pocket. I say thanks but no thanks, it's ok, it's hard to split a plum anyway, it'll be messy. 'I've got my apple,' I say. A few minutes later he holds out half a plum. 'Look, I managed to do it.' 'Oh,' I say. 'Ha, that's very kind but I still don't want the plum.' He drives me home. He asks if he can come inside and lie with me in my room. I say I'm sorry but I have ringworm, I can't touch anyone at the moment.

My ex-boyfriend says he's made a lot of money this month because he's been illegally renting out his apartment to a tourist on top of his regular job. I say I can't do that because I live with other people and my room is too messy. He says there is nothing stopping me from having a clean room and that I'm lazy. I say there are lots of things stopping me, and also I don't feel motivated by people criticising me. He says he has gently encouraged me to do things in the past but it didn't work, he needs to be harsher with me. He asks how old my housemates are and I say they are thirty-five and forty-five. He says that if someone can't afford to live alone by the time they are thirty-five, then there is something wrong with them. I say I won't be able to afford to live alone by thirty-five. 'Life is expensive, things aren't how they used to be,' I say. 'Why are you talking to me like I'm out of touch with how much it costs to rent these days,' he says. 'People need to work out how to be financially stable.' I say I won't ever be financially stable because I'm not healthy enough to work full-time and he says, 'I know but you need to think laterally, you need to work around it.' He asks me how much money I make a month. I tell him a figure and he says, 'Oh that's not very much.' He says he matched with this girl I used to work with on an online dating site, and that she has a foot fetish. 'You know who I'm talking about? Maryanne? She was always smirking.' 'Yes I know who you mean,' I say.

I'm trying to stop sleeping with a towering pile of clothes on my bed so now I'm sleeping with a towering pile of clothes on the floor instead. I ask my sister if we can hang out tomorrow, she says she's too busy. The next day she says she is driving two hours to pick up a fish tank for the axolotl she impulse-bought online.

I remember a guy I went on a date with who broke my umbrella by pushing large rocks off a rockpile with it. He said he would get me a new one but then he stopped talking to me. He was sleeping with other people while he was dating me but I didn't know that at the time. Deep down I think I knew what was happening but didn't say anything because his dad had cancer and I was trying to make allowances.

As soon as I get to the office the sales rep calls me. She says she just had an angry cafe manager telling her they'd received plain croissants instead of almond croissants about five times now. 'He said he told you about it last week, but I can't see it noted on the feedback sheet. Did you record it?' 'I can't remember,' I say, 'Maybe not.' She says we're going to lose him as a customer and she needs to talk to the manager about it but he'll ask why it wasn't noted by customer service staff on the feedback spreadsheet and why he's only just finding out about it. 'So, can you go through and find the note about the croissants on the feedback spreadsheet or else add it and backdate it.' 'Yep, no problem, I'll do that,' I say.

Me and the other new woman are printing out labels and laminating them. The labels don't align with the printer properly so the job takes a long time. 'I hate this,' she says. 'I got told to do this because apparently I didn't have enough to do, but I'm so behind on everything. The manager told me to scrub the stairs the other day when he thought I wasn't doing anything. That's not even my job? I have a bad back anyway.' 'Yeh that's pretty stupid,' I say. 'Do you know how important bees are?' she says. 'They're very important. I'm just about to start keeping bees. They're amazing. We really need to do more for the bees.' 'I agree, I think bees are really cool and important,' I say.

The accounts manager calls me into his office. 'Have you been on any dates this week,' he asks. 'No, I'm meeting someone next week though I think,' I say. 'He's thirty-eight.' 'How old are you,' he says. 'Twenty-eight,' I say. 'That's fine then isn't it,' he says. 'Yeh but it's my upper limit maybe, I want my kids to have a young father.' 'Hey, you never know what's going to happen,' the accounts manager says. 'My grandmother thought she was marrying a young healthy guy, they had four kids and then he died at thirty-two, and she lived to ninety-two.'

Some people like to have fun but that's not for me. I see my ex has abandoned his blog. When we broke up, he returned all the gifts I'd ever given him. In the end, the catalyst for the breakup was that I killed a fly with his DVD and he got angry. He asked me how my day was, I said I'd just killed a fly with the David Lynch DVD he'd given me to borrow. I thought it was a flippant and amusing remark but he said I was disrespectful. 'That's awful, that's something I gave you,' he said. 'How would you like it if I killed a fly with a book you gave me?' I said I wouldn't care, and if I did care, I would make a joke about it instead of ignoring me for five hours like he did.

I wake up two hours before my alarm goes off. At 6 a.m. I jump up and go to the courtyard and start pawing through the rubbish bin with my bare hands. I think I accidentally threw my opal earrings in the bin. They were wrapped in a tissue. I touch every single tissue in the bin but can't find them. I'm late to work. A lot of customers have missing orders and everyone keeps saying good morning. I feel attacked and afraid when I hear or read the words 'good morning'. I've never said 'good morning' to anyone in my life and I never will. The boss enters the office. His eyes pan down to see me eating an entire rockmelon and drinking from a cup that reads 'world's best boss'. He tries to make me follow the company Instagram account because they have 9,999 followers and he wants one more. I refuse. 'Hey I tried to call you just before,' he says. 'And there was no answer. Where were you?' I say I was probably in the toilet. 'If customers call and you're in the toilet, how are they going to place their bread orders?' I don't take a lunchbreak again. I stay at the office two hours after I am supposed to leave because I haven't printed all the stickers out for the bread bags and the sticker machine keeps jamming and if I don't print out the stickers for the packing team then the bread won't be delivered and hundreds of dollars' worth of bread will be wasted.

Two hours later I get home. My housemate asks me how my day was. I say it was long and stressful. I'm about to do yoga, you should do yoga with me, she says. I don't want to do yoga, I just want to sleep. I say I'm not sure I'll be very good at it because of the pain in my legs. She says I can adjust the positions. I say I kind of just want to lie down for a while to calm down and she says that yoga will help me calm down. 'I don't have a yoga mat,' I say. She says she has a spare one. Five minutes later we are on the living room floor on yoga mats and an American woman is on the TV screen doing yoga poses for us to copy. My legs hurt and I'm hungry.

The guy who got me the job rings me to chat. He asks how my night is going. I say that my housemate forced me to do yoga with her. 'Well, that's your fault for not saying no,' he says. 'You need to have better boundaries.' He asks me how I'm finding the job. 'It's a bit stressful,' I say. 'Why? It's not a hard job, you shouldn't find it stressful,' he says. 'Do you have anxiety problems or something?'

I wore big earrings with words written on them and a dress with a big collar to the art opening. I wanted people to look at the earrings and they did, but as soon as they looked at me I was embarrassed. Two people said they liked my earrings and one person said they liked my dress. I began to explain what was written on the earrings but my face was red and I couldn't look anyone in the eye. In the corner of the room I saw someone I went on a date with last year. He kept trying to get me to come to his house even though he lived on the opposite side of town. At a bar he told me his ex-girlfriend burnt all his clothes in a satanic ritual and that his art practice involved taking naked pictures of himself with an erection as a homage to some Dutch painter. He told me that he didn't ejaculate though, the erection was just for the picture.

I can't reply to my messages yet because I'm anaemic. The manager appeared at the office wearing tight lycra bike shorts and began to talk to me at length about croissants. I tried not to look at the bike shorts. He went to his office. I started making phone calls. I could hear him cackling loudly at something. I wanted to ask what was so funny but we don't have that kind of relationship. He's begun signing off group emails with an out-of-focus picture of wheat.

There must be more to life than who to blame. I felt calm when I saw a picture of grass growing through a blanket. I felt calm for the first time this year. The blanket was beige and looked like sand.

'Do you want to come over? I'll cook you dinner, it'll give me an excuse to drink.' When I get there he's starting on his second bottle of wine. Taking a sip of wine then vaping then chewing nicotine gum in quick succession. He is addicted to nicotine. I see he's using tinfoil to cook the salmon. I want to say that aluminium foil takes five hundred years to break down but I'm trying to be less critical so I don't say anything. He points out we have the same backpack and I already know this from stalking his Instagram account. He tells me I look too skinny, and that I should go to the gym. I say I can't go to the gym because of my inflammation. He says that is just an excuse and I should get buff like him. He pinches my arm. 'You have no muscle,' he says. He puts on a movie. 'I'm probably too drunk to have sex but we can kiss.' After ten minutes he asks if I want to have sex. I say yes. He unwraps a condom. I take my underwear off. 'Actually, I really want nicotine right now,' he says. I look up at him. 'Can it wait?' 'No.' He reaches for his vape and lies down next to me. He takes off the condom. He unwraps nicotine gum. 'Once I was having sex with this girl who I didn't want to have sex with. She had wanted to come to my house and in the middle of sex I said I wanted a cigarette and she got upset and left. But she didn't get that I didn't want to have sex with her so I had to do that.' 'Um,' I say. 'That seems mean.' 'No, it was good because she left and I got to have my cigarette.' 'Is that what happened with us just then?' I ask. He starts licking my nipples while chewing the nicotine gum. 'No, I like you, I just really wanted nicotine.'

On the phone a customer says she has received her Christmas grocery order but the order is completely wrong. 'We ordered ten packets of herbed spiced nuts but we only got five,' she says, 'We ordered twenty small Christmas puddings but we only received two, we ordered five large Christmas cakes but we got ten, there are five bags of granola which we didn't order at all, I don't know what they're doing here. Also last week we ordered ten packets of shortbread and five of them arrived broken, so you guys sent us out five replacement ones, but I've just opened the box now to see that four out of the five replacement packets are also broken.' 'Oh, that doesn't sound too good,' I say.

I don't get a break all shift. 'Did you print out those labels for those Christmas puddings,' the manager asks. 'Not yet, I've got quite a few things to finish first,' I say. 'The pudding labels are a priority though don't you think,' he says. 'We don't want people to miss out on getting puddings, I advertised them on Instagram.' He says he noticed I didn't finish all the emails in the inbox yesterday. He asks what happened. I say I stayed an hour past closing time but I couldn't finish everything in time. 'What were you doing though?' he says. I say I did the important emails and flagged the rest of the emails I ran out of time to do. 'Flagging doesn't work, you need to be more efficient, you need to be like a robot responding to emails,' he says.

The accounts manager asks if I want a ride home because he lives near me. I have to try and make small talk with him for thirty minutes. He asks what I'm doing for Christmas. 'Probably crying alone in my room,' I say. 'What? Are you serious?' he says. 'I'll probably go to the zoo alone for Christmas like I did last year,' I say. 'That sounds sad,' he says. 'No it's fine, I like being alone,' I say.

He says I should meet him in the city and we can go do something. I'm surprised he wants to do something. I take the bus into the city. When I arrive he messages to say he hasn't left yet, he says he'll meet me later. I walk around trying to decide where I should eat. I don't want anyone to see me eat though, I feel too earnest when a waitress asks me what food I want to eat.

'I like your outfit,' he says when he finally arrives. 'Thanks,' I say. 'Do you realise you look good right now?' he says. 'I mean, I like this dress,' I say. 'Well, good for you,' he says. I suggest going to a bar nearby and he says he doesn't like the look of it. He suggests going to a bar in another suburb thirty minutes away. 'But you only just got here,' I say. He says we could see a movie instead. We walk to the movie complex. All of the movies seem boring. 'What about that one?' I say. 'Actually, I don't really want to waste money on a movie anymore,' he says. We sit on a bench. 'Should we just go home?' he says. 'I don't know, I guess so,' I say.

Something falls on the ground and I don't pick it up. I could make soup and apply for another job but instead I am missing the person who ruined my life. I wore my Y2K nightgown to work again. I wondered if my boss could tell I slept in my clothes. The phone rang. It was a customer saying he'd ordered thirty bread rolls but he'd only received a delivery of three. The manager said, 'Busy weekend?' and I said, 'Well, I'm working here.' He said, 'Yeh, I mean the business – I'm not asking about your personal life.'

I keep giving work reasons to hate me because of the mistakes I am making and now that they've fired the other guy they hated, my shortcomings are more noticeable. Really, I just want to be in a ball pit in a McDonald's playground. I went to the doctor and he told me off for missing a medical appointment a few months back. He asked me why I didn't go. I said I had work. He said, 'Well, jobs come and go but your illness is forever.'

This turtleneck is choking me a little but it's the most excitement I've had for months so I should be grateful. I press a dirty tissue into a decorative seashell. I check to see if I'm still ugly.

I can't even sleep with anyone casually right now because I would need at least two weeks' notice to clean up my disgusting room. I don't want anyone to ask what I've been doing recently. What do you mean recently. Well, there was someone vaping in the abortion clinic waiting room. What else do you do with your time? I felt good when I collected seashells. That was the best part of the holiday.

I want more friends but I hate most people. I've always had enemies. My ex said he thought my enemy was cute! The last time we had sex there was a knock at the door. I got up and answered it. At the door was an old woman asking if the dead cat she'd just found was ours. I said we didn't have a cat. But I went to look at it anyway. I wished I could be in a relationship that didn't go downhill after one to three months. Blood was coming out of the cat's mouth. I went back to the bedroom. 'I just saw a dead cat, I don't think I'm in the mood anymore,' I said.

I consider my options. None of them seem appealing. I drive to the doctors and pass two people I hate. They're hugging. I eat dry cereal in the waiting room, sit on the wrong side of the seat. I tell the doctor I'm depressed. She says, 'But you can't be depressed, I saw you laughing last week.' She tells me that I should get another job and then I'll be happy. 'Have you thought about starting your own business?' I invent an allergy. I'm ready to love. But I can only do two things a day. My spare time isn't my spare time. I say I'm leaving the country soon. I need more bridges to burn. Every time someone tries to talk to me, I just say I'm leaving the country soon.

Returning home after a long day of doing nothing. Wearing neutral colours, not folding clothes, not doing dishes, not making an appointment. I eat porridge off a plate. I water the rubber plant that my mother has positioned behind the door because she hates it. It gets squashed every time the door opens.

My phone keeps accidentally calling people. I don't have any friends but it keeps calling my mother or the woman I did babysitting for two months ago. I am supposed to be meeting someone but my grandmother is dying. I'm walking around in the dark in a suburb very far from my house eating $1.62 worth of ham from a plastic bag. I can't remember what my skills are. My mother messages me to say that my grandmother is about to die, and then that she has died. I start typing out a message and my phone accidentally calls her. My mother says, 'I can't talk on the phone right now, I'm too upset, I just can't, I'll talk to you in a few days.' My phone accidentally calls her again, two more times. Summer is over and I didn't have fun. The mood ring I'm wearing is stuck on my finger.

Excerpts from this book have previously appeared in *The Nervous Breakdown, The Suburban Review, Turbine, Running Dog, X-R-A-Y, Going Down Swinging* and *The Fanzine*. Thanks to the editors of these publications.

Southern Latitudes

Southern Latitudes is a series published by Giramondo devoted to writers from the southern hemisphere. The list brings together works by writers from across the south, to explore the resonances and resemblances between their perspectives.

Mariana Dimópulos *All My Goodbyes* (fiction)
translated from Spanish by Alice Whitmore
Argentina
Ashleigh Young *Can You Tolerate This?* (essays)
New Zealand
Marcelo Cohen *Melodrome* (fiction)
translated from Spanish by Chris Andrews
Argentina
Mariana Dimópulos *Imminence* (fiction)
translated from Spanish by Alice Whitmore
Argentina
Norman Erikson Pasaribu *Sergius Seeks Bacchus* (poetry)
translated from Indonesian by Tiffany Tsao
Indonesia
Bruno Lloret *Nancy* (fiction)
translated from Spanish by Ellen Jones
Chile
Pip Adam *Nothing to See* (fiction)
New Zealand
Zarah Butcher-McGunnigle *Nostalgia Has Ruined My Life* (fiction)
New Zealand

About the author

Zarah Butcher-McGunnigle is a writer from Auckland, New Zealand. She is the author of *Autobiography of a Marguerite* (Hue & Cry Press, 2014).